Tilly the Tidy Puppy

Tilly often dreamed of tidying. Last night, she'd dreamed of gathering up the bowls on the bowling green where Anna's grandad played. And she'd dreamed of tidying up the ducks in the park.

But now Tilly's tidying had got her into really big trouble. There was only one thing for it – she would have to stop!

Titles in Jenny Dale's PUPPY TALES™ series

All of Jenny Dale's PUPPY TALES books can
be ordered at your local bookshop or are
available by post from Book Service by Post
(tel: 01624 675137)

Jenny Dale's
PUPPY
TALES™

Tilly the Tidy Puppy

by Jenny Dale

Illustrated by Frank Rodgers

A Working Partners Book

MACMILLAN CHILDREN'S BOOKS

Special thanks to Ali Ives

First published 1999 by Macmillan Children's Books
a division of Pan Macmillan Limited
20 New Wharf Road, London N1 9RR
Basingstoke and Oxford
www.panmacmillan.com

Associated companies throughout the world

Created by Working Partners Limited
London W12 7QY

ISBN 0 330 37366 8

7 9 8

A CIP catalogue record for this book is available from
the British Library.

Typeset by SX Composing DTP, Rayleigh, Essex
Printed and bound in Great Britain by Mackays of Chatham plc, Kent

Chapter One

"Hello, Tilly, I'm home!" Anna called.

Tilly, Anna Drew's collie pup, leapt down the stairs and straight into her owner's arms. "I've missed you!" she barked. "Why do you have to go to school?"

Anna gave Tilly a cuddle. "Have

you been good today?" she asked.

Tilly snuffled at Anna's neck, making her laugh. "Oh, yes, I've been very busy, tidying up."

"I do hope you haven't been tidying *again*," said Anna, as she walked into the living room. "We can never find anything these days."

Whoops, Tilly thought. She snuggled even closer to Anna, hoping she wasn't about to be told off – *again*! "It's not my fault," she woofed. "It's just the way I am. I'm from a sheepdog family – and sheepdogs like to tidy."

But Anna wasn't listening. She was looking for something. "*Tilly*," she said sternly. "What have you done with the TV remote control?" She put Tilly down on the carpet and started searching the room.

Remote control . . . Tilly thought hard.

"I left it on the sofa this morning," Anna muttered. "Where have you put it, Tilly?"

Tilly wagged her tail. "Oh," she woofed, "you mean that plastic box with the buttons on it! Yes, I did tidy it up. Now, where did I put it . . . ?"

Tilly was still thinking when Mrs Drew walked past the living room, carrying shopping bags into the kitchen.

"Hello, Tilly," she called. "I hope you've been good."

Tilly padded out to say hello.

Mrs Drew had dropped the bags of shopping all over the kitchen floor. And to Tilly's annoyance, she seemed more interested in making herself a cup of tea than in putting the shopping away.

Just then, there was a ringing noise from the living room. Anna called out, "Mum – it's for you!"

Mrs Drew put down the teapot and walked past Tilly into the living room.

Tilly watched from the doorway as Mrs Drew laughed and chattered about this and that. Tilly just couldn't understand why people spent so much time talking to what looked like a plastic bone.

Mrs Drew talked for so long that Tilly thought she would never stop. *Well, I suppose I'll just have to tidy up the shopping*, she thought.

Tilly wandered back into the kitchen and stuck her head into the nearest carrier bag. It didn't look very exciting.

She had a sniff, then wrinkled her nose. Tilly knew those smells.

They belonged in the bathroom upstairs. And they reminded her of the vet's (Tilly hated going there). Still, whatever it smelled like, it all had to be put away.

Tilly grabbed the bag with her teeth and began tugging it out of the kitchen, along the hallway and up the stairs. It wasn't easy for her – she was still quite a small puppy.

On the landing, some of the bottles and tubes fell out of the bag, but at last Tilly managed to get it into the bathroom. She placed it neatly against a wall and then went back to collect the strays.

Just as she'd been taught by

her mum, a champion sheepdog, Tilly kept low to the ground, rounding them up one by one, then nudging them towards the bathroom to join the others.

However, there was one stray plastic bottle which simply wouldn't do as it was told, so Tilly growled and nipped at it gently. That should have been enough to bring it into line – but not this one, oh no!

Tilly nipped it again, harder. A green smelly liquid began to seep out of it. It dripped onto the landing carpet.

"Uh-oh," Tilly whimpered nervously. "That wasn't supposed to happen." Tilly began to wish that she'd never picked *this* bag.

But she'd started, so she'd have to finish.

Leaving a gooey trail of green slime on the carpet, Tilly continued onwards to the bathroom, nudging the difficult bottle with her nose.

"*Til-ly*, what *are* you doing?" called Anna, still downstairs watching TV.

"Nothing," Tilly barked back innocently. She sounded a bit strange because she was trying her hardest not to get the awful green slime in her mouth.

At last Tilly got the leaking bottle into the bathroom and placed it neatly by the bag. Wagging her tail she stared proudly at her work. Perfect – if you didn't count the green slime on the carpet . . .

Tilly had spotted one more stray on the stairs that needed fetching. She scampered after it.

"Come along," Tilly growled quietly as she picked up the last white box with her teeth, "time to join the rest of the flock."

Trotting back along the landing,

Tilly's tummy rumbled. Thinking that it was nearly time for her supper, Tilly forgot about the green oozy slime – until she slipped on it.

Tilly's teeth gripped the box in surprise. The top popped off and clouds of white powder flew everywhere! *"Who-oaa!"* she yelped as she landed on her back.

Anna and Mrs Drew rushed up the stairs to see what was going on.

"What a mess!" exclaimed Mrs Drew. She looked very annoyed.

"I'm *soooo* sorry," Tilly whined, rolling over and over on the carpet, trying to get the powder out of her coat.

Anna was trying not to laugh. "Tilly, you look like a ghost!" she giggled.

Tilly decided that she'd better have a really good shake.

But Mrs Drew picked up the puppy by the scruff of her neck. "Oh no you don't!" she said, wagging a finger crossly. "You're not making any more mess. You're going straight in the bath – and after that you can stay in the kitchen, out of my way!"

"Don't be mad, Mum," pleaded Anna. "I bet Tilly was just trying to tidy up. She's always doing that."

Tilly stared up at Mrs Drew and whimpered, "I really am sorry." But for once even Tilly's big

brown eyes couldn't melt Mrs Drew's heart.

"She's gone too far this time," Mrs Drew said firmly. "It's about time Tilly went back to the farm!"

Chapter Two

That evening, Tilly lay curled up
in her basket, trembling with
misery. Even though her mum
still lived at the farm, Tilly didn't
want to go back there. She lived
with Anna now and wanted to
stay with her.

Tilly loved Anna, and she was

sure Anna loved her too. She was always saying so, and kissing and cuddling and tickling Tilly.

Tilly whined softly, feeling very sorry for herself. She hadn't meant to make a mess. She *hated* mess! Tilly's mum would understand. Being a sheepdog, she was a tidier too, just like the rest of Tilly's family. It was in

their blood. Collies made such good sheepdogs because they *liked* to tidy up.

Tilly often dreamed of tidying. Last night, she'd dreamed of gathering up the bowls on the bowling green where Anna's grandad played. And she'd dreamed of tidying up the ducks in the park.

But now Tilly's tidying had got her into really big trouble. There was only one thing for it – she would have to stop.

If I can't tidy, I'll have to find something else to do, Tilly thought. *I know! I could gather up leaves in the garden!*

She sat up, feeling much more cheerful – then slumped down

again. No, that wouldn't work. Gathering was just like tidying. It was a different word, but it meant the same.

"There must be *something* I can do," she yapped to herself. She scratched an itch behind her ear with her back leg. "The problem is, I don't seem to be able to do anything except tidy, and I don't even do *that* very well."

While Tilly was banished to the kitchen, Anna sat in the living room with her mum and dad. She tried to convince them that Tilly was trying her best. "Tilly doesn't mean to be naughty," she said anxiously. "She just can't help tidying things up."

Mr Drew looked worried. "Perhaps choosing a collie as a pet was a bad idea," he said. "Maybe Tilly should have stayed at the farm, to work as a sheepdog."

Anna shook her head. "Tilly loves it here!" she cried. "And she'll soon settle down and stop causing so much trouble."

"I wish we could be so sure," said Mrs Drew. "Tilly's very sweet, but her sheepdog instincts are very strong. She even tries to round *us* up when we go out for a walk."

Anna giggled. Her mum was right. Tilly tidied everything, and if you got in the way she tidied you up as well. Last weekend, she'd been in trouble for chasing Grandad's prize-winning hens and their chicks around his garden!

Sighing, Anna got up to go and check on her disgraced puppy.

Tilly's heart pounded when she saw the door handle turn. She still hadn't thought of a job that she could do, and she desperately wanted to show Mr and Mrs Drew that she was sorry.

The door creaked open, and Anna came into the room. Tilly yelped with relief.

"*Shhh*," Anna whispered, then picked up one of Tilly's rubber balls and opened the back door.

"I didn't mean to be naughty," Tilly woofed as she ran around

Anna's ankles, waiting for her to throw the ball. "I was trying to be good!"

"Oh Tilly, you really must learn to do as you're told," Anna said as she threw Tilly's ball on to the grass.

Tilly fetched the ball and put it back down by Anna's feet. "I will try, I promise," she woofed, wagging her tail happily. "Throw it again, Anna!"

"Last time," said Anna, throwing the ball as far as she could. It landed smack in the middle of Mr Drew's best rose bed.

Tilly raced after it.

"No, Tilly, not there!" Anna shouted. "It's too muddy and – *stay*!"

But Tilly wasn't listening. She grabbed the ball and bounded back past Anna, towards the kitchen.

"*Til-ly*!" Anna shouted. "*Stop*!"

Tilly did stop – but not until she was in the middle of the kitchen floor.

Anna didn't know whether to laugh or cry. Tilly had left mucky pawprints all over the newly washed floor. If her mum saw them, Anna knew she would go up the wall. "*Til-ly – sit*!" she hissed, trying to be as quiet as possible.

"What's the matter, Anna?" Tilly woofed. She didn't understand what Anna wanted her to do.

"Tilly – be quiet and sit still. I

need to clean your paws."

But when Anna brought out the towel, Tilly thought it was another game.

"*Grrrrr*," she growled as she grabbed hold of one end of the towel and tussled with it.

"What is going on?" said Mrs Drew as she walked into the kitchen. She stopped and stared at the floor.

"I can explain, Mum," mumbled Anna. "As soon as I've tidied up, I'll come and explain."

"I don't want any more explanations and excuses," said Mrs Drew angrily. "I've had enough, I really have. Tilly is going back to the farm first thing tomorrow!"

Chapter Three

Tilly slept badly that night. She had nightmares about untidy piles of bones and untidy piles of knickers and socks. She tried hard to ignore them, all spread out so messily, but in the end she couldn't help herself – she *had* to tidy them up!

When Tilly woke early the next morning, she remembered – she was being taken back to the farm today.

Tilly could hardly believe it. She had decided never, ever to tidy up again – but now it was too late.

"Morning, Tilly," said Anna as she opened the kitchen door. She poured some puppy-meal into a bowl and placed it on the floor. "Eat up," she said. "We've got to go to the farm soon."

But Tilly wasn't hungry. She didn't want to go. What if she was never allowed to see Anna again? It would break her heart. "Please don't send me away, Anna," she whimpered. But Anna didn't even look upset.

"Ready?" asked Mr Drew after they'd all had breakfast.

"Tilly hasn't eaten her breakfast," said Anna, looking anxious.

"Oh, well," said Mr Drew. "We'll take some puppy biscuits for her to nibble on the way." He fastened Tilly's lead to her collar and then handed it to Anna.

Mr Drew opened the front door and went out to the car. Tilly knew she was supposed to follow, but this was her last chance to plead for forgiveness.

"*I don't want to go!*" she howled as she dug her paws into the carpet. "*Please don't make me!*"

But Anna didn't listen. She picked Tilly up and carried her

out to the car. "Come on, Tilly. Please don't make this even more difficult," she pleaded. "It's for the best."

Tilly and Anna sat in the back of the car as Mr Drew drove them across town and out into the countryside. Usually Tilly loved to see the fields and large open spaces, hoping she'd get the chance for a good run. But not today. Today Tilly wished she'd been allowed to stay at home.

"Here we are then," said Mr Drew as he pulled into the farm car park. "Hold on tight to Tilly," he told Anna, "and we'll go and enrol."

Tilly followed Anna and Mr Drew as they walked to the farmhouse – and then carried on right past it! Perhaps they weren't taking her back, after all! Tilly allowed her tail to wag, just a little.

Anna led her down a muddy path, past a tall hedge and into a field where there were lots of other people with puppies. Tilly had never seen so many people with puppies in one place. She became very excited.

"Hello," she barked. "What are you all doing here?"

"Search me," woofed a terrier pup with a grumpy-looking face. "One minute I was happily gnawing on the dining-room table, and the next thing I know I'm being dragged into this field. Bit of a cheek if you ask me!"

"Actually, we're all here for obedience classes," yapped a spaniel puppy.

"*What* classes?" Tilly woofed, puzzled.

"Obedience classes," the spaniel yapped again. "You know – sit, walk, fetch, stay – all that sort of thing!"

"You mean we're going to find out what all that stuff means?" asked Tilly, who had heard those words before but never understood them.

"That's right, slowcoach," said an Alsatian puppy.

Tilly couldn't believe her luck. She might not have to leave Anna after all. She just had to go to . . . obedience classes!

Just then, someone gave Tilly a pat. She turned round to see a pair of green boots. When she looked up, Tilly saw it was her mum's owner, Mrs Wagg!

"Hello, Tilly," Mrs Wagg said. "Haven't you grown?"

"Hello," woofed Tilly, tail wagging. "I'm here for your

obedience class – and I'm very excited!" She leapt up and down, yapping happily, her muddy paws covering Mrs Wagg's jeans in brown splodges.

All the other owners looked at Tilly and frowned. She really was a very badly behaved puppy.

Anna was very embarrassed.

"Get down, Tilly!" she said sternly.

"What?" barked Tilly, as she carried on leaping up and down.

"Well, Anna," said Mrs Wagg laughing, "I can see why you've brought Tilly along to my class!"

Tilly watched as Mrs Wagg led a grown-up collie into the middle of the field.

"Welcome to my obedience classes," Mrs Wagg said. "This is one of my sheepdogs – Jed."

Jed woofed a greeting, and most of the puppies got very excited and started barking too.

"Over the next few weeks your puppies will learn to understand what you want them to do," said Mrs Wagg.

Tilly gave another little yelp of excitement.

"They will learn when you want them to sit, to lie down, to stay, and to walk to heel," said Mrs Wagg. "Soon they will be well behaved at all times."

Mr Drew raised an eyebrow, and a couple of other owners tittered. Tilly wondered whether their puppies were really badly behaved too.

"So first of all, let's see good behaviour in action," said Mrs Wagg. "Jed is going to demonstrate." She looked at Jed, who was standing by her side. "Jed – *sit*!"

Jed sat, and all the owners clapped.

Tilly sat down too – in surprise!
"So that's what Anna means
when she asks me to sit," she
woofed thoughtfully.

"Now, Jed – *down*!" said Mrs
Wagg firmly.

Jed lay on the ground. And once
again everyone clapped.

Tilly was very impressed. She
was going to learn a lot in Mrs
Wagg's class.

"Jed – *stay*!" said Mrs Wagg. She
walked away towards the
puppies, leaving Jed where he
was.

Jed didn't follow Mrs Wagg. He
lay on the ground, waiting and
watching.

"Jed – *come*!" Mrs Wagg called.
Jed didn't need to be called twice!

He raced over to Mrs Wagg and sat down in front of her.

Then Mrs Wagg placed a ball on the ground next to Jed. Tilly wanted to bound over and grab the ball, but Anna was holding her lead tightly.

Jed bent and sniffed at the ball, but Mrs Wagg said, "*Off*, Jed, *off*!"

Jed left the ball alone.

Wow! thought Anna. *I wonder if I could teach Tilly to leave the remote control alone?*

"Over the next few weeks, all your puppies will be learning these commands," said Mrs Wagg. "But now, it's back to the beginning. Jed – *sit*!"

Mrs Wagg and Jed performed

the sit command a few more times.

Tilly looked up at Anna, then back at Jed. "I could easily do that one," she woofed.

"Now, it's your turn," said Mrs Wagg, looking around her class.

Tilly couldn't wait. "Ask me, Anna! Ask me!" she barked. "I can do it, I know I can!"

"Be quiet, Tilly," hissed Anna, feeling very embarrassed. None of the other puppies were making a noise. Then she took a deep breath and said, "Tilly – *sit*!" just like Mrs Wagg.

And to Anna's surprise, Tilly sat – beautifully.

"Well!" said Mr Drew, who was standing at the side of the field with some other spectators.

"Good girl, Tilly!" said Mrs
Wagg when she saw Tilly sitting.

"Oh Tilly, you clever girl!" said
Anna, kneeling to give Tilly a
cuddle.

Tilly gave her a happy lick.
"Nothing to it," she woofed
happily. "It was easy-peasy!"

Chapter Four

Again and again the puppies were asked to sit. Tilly noticed that some of the other puppies were still doing it all wrong. They weren't listening or sitting when they were supposed to. They were making a terrible mess of it.

Next to her was a Yorkie, who

kept jumping up when his owner asked him to sit.

Tilly couldn't help herself. She pulled Anna over to the Yorkie. "*This* is what you're supposed to do," Tilly told him. She plonked her bottom down on the ground to demonstrate exactly how to sit properly.

"Leave me alone!" the Yorkie barked. Although he was a little dog, his shrill bark was very loud!

"Come away, Tilly," Anna said crossly, yanking Tilly's lead. "What's the matter? A few minutes ago you were being so good."

Tilly was just about to sit again, when she spotted a Dalmatian puppy doing everything wrong too. The puppy wasn't even trying to sit when she was told. She just wanted to chat to the spaniel puppy next to her.

"No! No! No!" woofed Tilly, jumping up to attract their attention. "You're supposed to be *sitting* – like this, OK?"

But neither of the puppies paid any attention to her. Using all her strength, Tilly dragged Anna towards them.

"Can't you keep your dog under control?" moaned the spaniel puppy's owner as Tilly accidentally barged into her.

Anna went pink. "Sorry," she mumbled.

"What a badly behaved puppy," whispered the Dalmatian's owner to the boy next to him. "Much worse than my Dapple!" They both looked at Tilly and shook their heads.

Anna managed to drag Tilly back to her place, just as Mrs Wagg announced that it was the end of the class.

"Maybe we shouldn't bother bringing Tilly to another class," said Mr Drew as they were walking to the car. "After the first five minutes, she didn't seem to pay attention."

"Oh, she did," Anna said, "but then all the other puppies distracted her when they misbehaved!"

Tilly woofed, pleased that Anna understood.

Mr Drew laughed. "From what I saw," he said, "Tilly was doing most of the misbehaving!"

"But watch this!" said Anna as they reached the car. "Tilly – *sit*!"

Tilly sat.

Anna smiled proudly at her dad.

"OK," said her dad, grinning. "Maybe Tilly did learn something, after all."

Chapter Five

The following Saturday, Tilly
arrived at the farm for her next
obedience class. This time she was
determined not to be distracted
by the other puppies, whatever
they were doing.

  "I hope you've all been
practising the sit command," said

Mrs Wagg. "This week we're going to teach the puppies to stay. I'll demonstrate with Jed."

Mrs Wagg walked a little further away with the sheepdog and told him to sit. Then she told him to stay while she walked a few paces away from him.

The collie sat still and alert, watching Mrs Wagg with his sharp brown eyes.

After a few seconds, Mrs Wagg beckoned Jed to her. "*Come*, Jed!" she called. Jed leapt up and ran to Mrs Wagg who praised him as everyone clapped.

"Now it's your turn," Mrs Wagg told the class.

To begin with, Tilly did exactly as she was told. She sat, then stayed where she was while Anna walked away. But then she noticed that most of the other puppies were not staying at all. They were running here, there and everywhere. What a mess!

"Come back, everyone!" Tilly woofed. "That isn't how you stay! Come back!"

Tilly was making more noise than all of the other puppies, but still they wouldn't listen to her.

"*Tilly – BE QUIET!*" Mrs Wagg's booming voice silenced Tilly. "We're tired of hearing you!"

Mrs Wagg looked around at the puppies, who were all looking at her. "Now, let's try it again . . . Puppies – *sit!*"

All the puppies sat – and some even stayed while their owners walked away from them.

By the end of the class, all the puppies could do the stay command perfectly, and their owners were feeling extremely proud.

"Right, before we finish, let's give the stay command a real test," said Mrs Wagg, looking at her watch. "This time I'd like the puppies to stay at the bottom of the field while their owners walk right back up to the top."

"All that way?" Anna whispered to the girl next to her. "I hope Tilly does as she's told."

"Of course I will!" Tilly woofed up at her.

All the puppies waited at the bottom of the field while their owners walked away from them. Tilly's heart was beating fast. This was her big chance to show Anna and Mr Drew how well she could behave. She was going to do what she was told and she wasn't going to be distracted – even if all the other puppies went completely wild.

"Bet I can beat you back to my

owner when we're called!" Tyson the Yorkie yapped to Tilly.

"Bet you can't!" Tilly woofed back.

"OK – on their command, race you!" barked Tyson.

Suddenly there was a deep frightening rumble in the sky. All the puppies crouched down in alarm.

Anna stared up at the clouds.

"What a wonderful old plane!" Mr Drew called from the edge of the field. "I haven't seen one of those for years. It must be on its way to an air show."

Spying the crowd in the field below him, the pilot flew lower, showing off his flying skills.

"Help! It's a monster – and it's

coming to get us!" the puppies all yelped, panicking.

"Stay calm!" called Mrs Wagg, sensing their fear. But she was so far away and the plane was so noisy that the puppies couldn't hear her.

"Better make a run for it!" one of them whimpered.

The others yelped their agreement. Scattering across the field, the puppies ran like crazy to escape the scary noise, which was getting louder and louder.

They hid in rabbit holes and ditches. They hid under bushes and behind fallen logs and trees. Some even hid as far away as the edge of the wood. Soon there was only one puppy in sight!

Chapter Six

Tilly hadn't run. She lay crouched close to the ground, waiting for Anna. She didn't know what the huge scary thing in the sky was either, but she was determined to wait for Anna's command.

"Dapple, where are you?" Tilly heard a voice shout, as all the puppies' owners came running back down the field.

"Patch – come back!"

"Tyson! Here, boy! Tyson!"

Then Tilly heard Anna's voice. "Oh, good girl, Tilly!" Anna was rushing towards her. "All the other puppies have run away."

Tilly wagged her tail proudly as Anna praised her, but she couldn't forget all her new friends. "What if they get lost?" she woofed.

"I don't know how we are going to gather all the puppies together again," Mrs Wagg said worriedly.

Tilly's ears pricked up. The puppies needed to be gathered – that meant *tidied*! Tilly was very good at that. "Let me help find them," she woofed. "I could round them up, I'm sure."

But no one was listening. They were far too busy panicking, so Tilly decided she would go and find the puppies by herself. Barking loudly, she ran off down the field.

"Come back, Tilly!" called Anna. "*Stay!*"

But just this once, Tilly was not going to obey. She was going to rescue the other puppies – and make Anna even more proud of her.

In the long grass at the side of the field, Tilly picked up Dapple the Dalmatian's scent straight away. "Hello there, Dapple," she woofed. "The scary thing in the sky has gone now. We're safe!"

The Dalmatian poked her head out of a rabbit hole. "Oh Tilly, am I pleased to see you!" she barked.

"Come along then," Tilly woofed. "I'll take you back to your owner before I go and find the others."

No one could believe it when Tilly came bounding back,

bringing Dapple with her. Anna looked at Mrs Wagg, and Mr Drew seemed amazed.

Dapple's owner rushed over and scooped up his puppy. "Oh, thank goodness!" the boy cried. "I thought you were lost!"

The Dalmatian yelped joyfully, wagging her tail. "Thanks, Tilly!" she barked over her owner's shoulder.

But Tilly was already disappearing back into the long grass. "Won't be long," she woofed.

The next scent Tilly found belonged to Tyson the Yorkie. The little pup with the loud bark was hiding behind a fallen tree, and he was still shaking with fear.

"It's safe to come out now, Tyson," woofed Tilly kindly. "Follow me, I'll take you back to your owner."

This time, when Tilly emerged bringing another puppy with her, Mrs Wagg began clapping. "Do you realise what Tilly is doing?" Mrs Wagg said.

Anna nodded and smiled. "She's leading the puppies back to their owners!"

Mrs Wagg laughed. "She's tidying them all up!"

"Well done, Tilly!" everyone called. "Keep up the good work!"

"You bet!" woofed Tilly, as she left Tyson with his happy owner. "Be back with the next one soon." And once again she ran back down the field. "This is much, much better than tidying up Mrs Drew's shopping," she woofed to herself. "This is wonderful fun!"

Dapple, Tyson, Patch . . .
Digby, Tess, Hunter . . .
Brandy, Lady, Sheba . . .

On and on Tilly went – until, finally, she had rounded up all the missing puppies. As she led Bouncer, the last puppy, back to his owner, everyone cheered and clapped even louder than before.

Tired but happy, Tilly trotted over to Anna, who picked her up and hugged her tight. "I'm *so* proud of you, Tilly," she whispered.

The next day, Tilly and Anna

stood in the garden at home, watching as Mr Drew carried a big bag out onto the lawn.

What's in there? Tilly wondered, her nose twitching.

Mr Drew grinned at Tilly then tipped out the contents of the bag onto the grass. Tilly's ears pricked up in surprise as balls of every size and colour fell out of the bag and bounced across the lawn.

"Wow!" she yelped.

Anna laughed. "Every owner at the obedience class has given you a ball, Tilly," she explained. "As a thank you."

"And free lessons from Mrs Wagg," added Mr Drew, "as a special thank you for saving the day."

Anna picked up a ball and threw it. It landed *smack* in the middle of Mr Drew's rose bed.

Tilly was just about to chase after it when Anna said firmly, "No, Tilly – *stay*!"

"OK," Tilly woofed, and stayed by Anna's side while Mr Drew rescued the ball.

"Well done, Tilly," said Anna proudly as she threw another ball – but into the middle of the lawn this time!

Tilly raced down the garden and brought the stray ball back to the pile on the lawn.

"It looks like Tilly has learnt a lot since she started the obedience classes," said Mrs Drew, coming into the garden to watch.

"She certainly has," said Anna proudly. "She'll never be called the naughtiest puppy in the class again!"

And as Anna laughed and threw one ball after another around the lawn, Tilly thought she was in tidying heaven!